Wand in
the Pond

Wand in the Pond

Lucy Mayflower

Hodder
Children's
Books

a division of Hachette Children's Books

Special thanks to Lucy Courtenay

Created by Hodder Children's Books and Lucy Courtenay
Text and illustrations copyright © 2006 Hodder Children's Books
Illustrations created by Artful Doodlers

First published in Great Britain in 2006
by Hodder Children's Books

5

A Catalogue record for this book is available from the British Library

ISBN – 10: 0 340 91178 6
ISBN – 13: 9780340911785

Printed and bound in Great Britain
by Bookmarque Ltd, Croydon, Surrey

The paper and board used in this paperback by Hodder Children's Books
are natural recyclable products made from wood grown in
sustainable forests. The manufacturing processes conform to the
environmental regulations of the country of origin.

Hodder Children's Books
A division of Hachette Children's Books
338 Euston Rd, London NW1 3BH

Contents

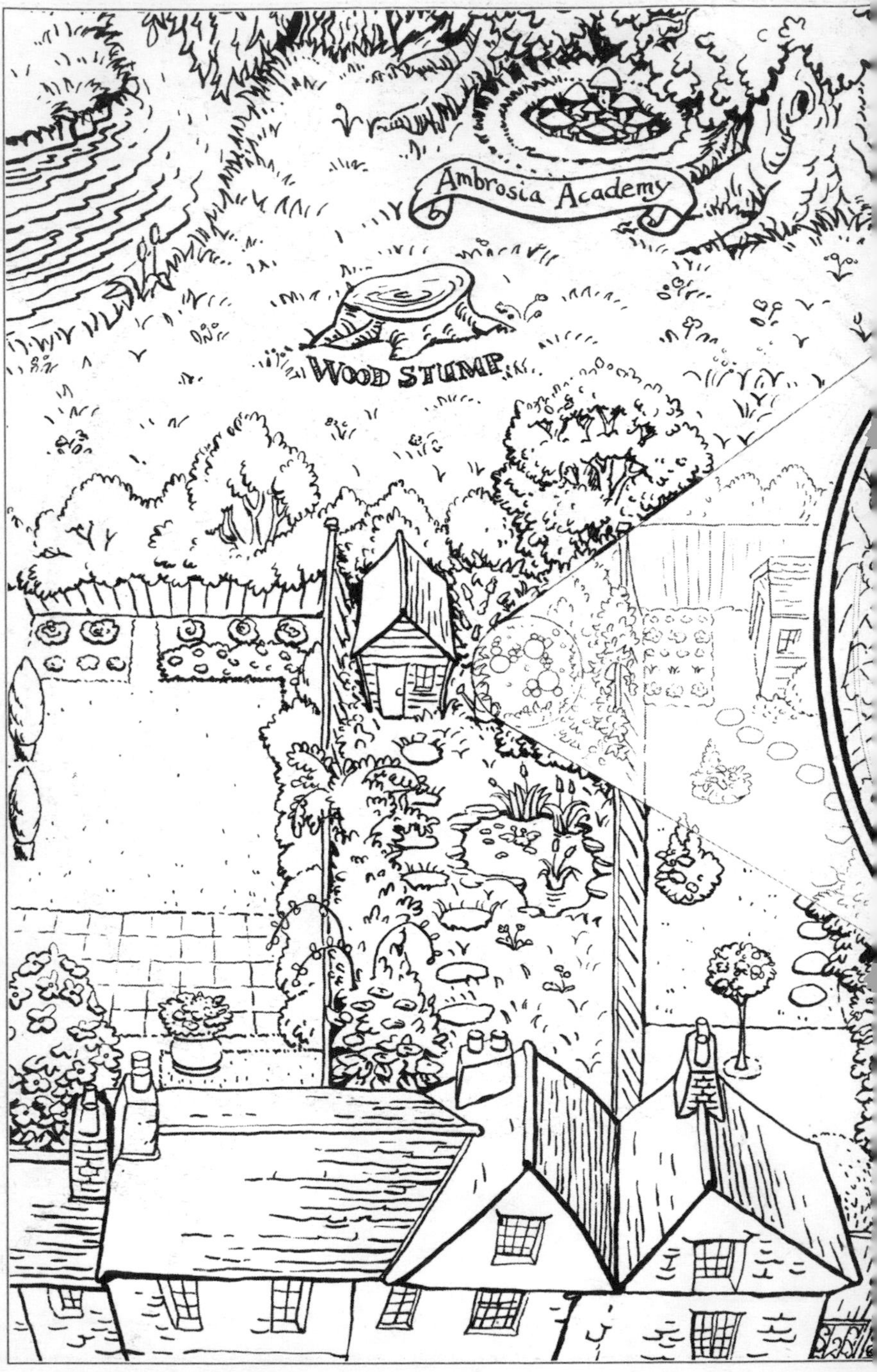

Ambrosia Academy
WOOD STUMP

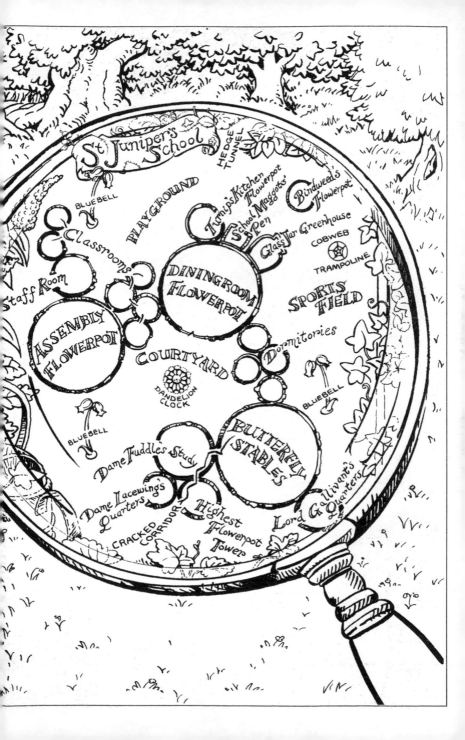

1

Ping

Down at the bottom of the garden, the fairies were waiting. They stood in rows in the courtyard and on the flowerpot towers of St Juniper's, and stared up at the sky.

St Juniper's, the famous school for fairies, was expecting a new pupil. And she was late.

The Head of St Juniper's, Dame Fuddle, looked at the dandelion clock in the middle of St Juniper's courtyard. Half the seeds were missing already.

"I don't understand it!" Dame Fuddle said. She twisted her hands together. "The signals in the stars last night were very clear! She was coming today! At

dawn! At a quarter past the dandelion!
And now it's half past the dandelion
and she's not here!"

Dame Fuddle often spoke in
exclamation marks.

The dandelion clock lost another seed.

"Now what are we going to do?" Dame Fuddle said. "We always welcome new fairies this way!"

"We can't keep our fairies out here all morning," said Dame Lacewing, Dame Fuddle's deputy. Dame Lacewing taught Fairy Maths, and was the scariest teacher at St Juniper's. "They have lessons to go to."

All the fairies started chattering with excitement. If the new fairy was *really* late, maybe they wouldn't have lessons at all.

High above the courtyard, five fairies sat on the highest flowerpot tower and dangled their feet over the edge. A very hairy bumblebee zoomed around above them. Although it was a long way down, the view was excellent. They could see St Juniper's Butterfly Stables, and Sports Field, and Strawberry Patch.

Behind them, they could see right over the Weeds and the Watering Can. They could even see all the way across the Pond. And a very long way in the distance, they could see the huge and enormous House.

The sky stayed grey and cloudy and totally empty.

"This is a perfect place for raindrop bombs," said the blonde, short-haired fairy sitting closest to the edge of the flowerpot tower. Two tiny spiders dangled from her ears, and she had a smudge of raspberry jam on her cheek.

"Good idea, Nettle," said the fairy next to her. "They'd land on Dame Fuddle's head if you got the angle right." She took two honeycakes out of her pocket, and ate one.

The red-haired, cross-looking fairy on the other side of Nettle reached out and grabbed the second honeycake. "I'll have that, Tiptoe," she said. "Flea needs some catching practice."

"It would be nice if you said 'please',
Kelpie," Tiptoe complained.

"Would it?" said Kelpie. She threw the
honeycake into the air. The hairy
bumblebee above them buzzed down
and caught it.

"How would we get the raindrops up
here?" asked a dark-haired fairy
stroking a fat green caterpillar lying on
her lap.

"Rain falls from the sky, stupid,"
Kelpie said sarcastically. "It doesn't
start on the ground. You do ask thick
questions sometimes, Sesame."

"Stop being so grumpy, Kelpie," said
Sesame. "I know it's early, but we had
to get out of bed too, you know."

The prettiest fairy stopped plaiting
her wild, curly hair. "We'll get an acorn
cup up here to catch the rain," she said.
"Then we'll get a blade of grass and fix
it so we can slide the raindrops out of

the acorn cup, down the blade and splat! Raindrop bombs! That's my most brilliant idea ever." She gave a brilliant smile.

Nettle frowned. "It wasn't *your* idea, Brilliance," she said.

Brilliance shrugged. "An idea is useless without a plan."

"Who says I don't have a plan?" Nettle demanded.

"You never have plans, Nettle," Brilliance said.

"Shall we do it tonight, Brilliance?" Tiptoe asked.

"It's going to rain later, Brilliance," Sesame added.

"Ooh, Brilliance, you are brilliant," said Kelpie.

"That's not fair!" Nettle glared at Brilliance. "You always take my ideas."

"Get over yourself, Nettle," Brilliance said. She preened her wings and looked up at the brightening sky. "I think the new fairy's coming at last."

"Don't change the subject!" Nettle shouted. The spiders on her ears bounced up and down nervously.

There was a ripple of excitement down in the courtyard. Everyone turned to look as a tiny black speck zoomed over the fence and hovered by the Pond.

"Wow!" Sesame breathed. "Is she riding an Emperor dragonfly?"

"Anyone can ride an Emperor dragonfly," said Kelpie. "Riding a bee is much harder."

The new fairy dug her knees into the dragonfly's sides. Everyone gasped as the dragonfly plummeted downwards, then stopped dead. The new fairy stood up on the dragonfly's back and did a somersault before landing neatly on the dragonfly's back again.

"That looked pretty hard to me," said Tiptoe.

"It's easy," said Brilliance confidently.

"When did you ever ride a
dragonfly?" Nettle demanded. She was
still angry about the raindrop bombs.

"Don't get your wings in a whizz,
Nettle," said Brilliance. "It's all about

balance, and I'm brilliant at balancing."

The fairy on the Emperor dragonfly shot into the air and looped the loop. Sesame squealed and covered her eyes. Tiptoe's mouth hung open. Even Kelpie looked impressed, a bit.

"Come on," said Brilliance. "Let's go and join the welcome party. It's boring up here."

She flexed her wings and jumped off the tower. Tiptoe and Sesame followed her, carrying Sprout the caterpillar between them. Kelpie whistled at Flea and jumped on his back.

Nettle stayed on the tower. "You're the boring one, Brilliance!" she shouted.

"Stay up here, then," Brilliance said. "I don't care."

"I will!" Nettle yelled. "I will, I will, I will!"

Brilliance and the others swooped down to the courtyard, leaving Nettle

alone on the flowerpot tower.

"I hate you, Brilliance!" Nettle turned three angry somersaults in a row to make herself feel better.

"Nice somersaults," said a voice.

Nettle spun round. The huge Emperor

dragonfly was hovering by the edge of the flowerpot tower. The dragonfly's wings were like silver and its body flashed blue and green. It was hovering so smoothly that it didn't seem to be moving at all.

The fairy on the dragonfly's back was staring at Nettle with interest. She was slim and neat, with slanting eyes and jet black hair which stuck straight up in the air.

"Nice somersaults," said the fairy again. "Can you do more than three in a row? I'm Ping."

"So?" said Nettle furiously. Ping patted the dragonfly's head. "And this is Pong," she said. "Watch this." Ping kicked Pong and zoomed backwards into a complicated figure of eight above the Pond. Nettle

noticed a gleam of silver falling through the air and landing in the Pond with a silent splash. Ping didn't seem to notice. She flew straight over Nettle's head with a little wave. Nettle gave Ping her best glare.

Pong the dragonfly rocketed down to the courtyard and stopped in front of

Dame Fuddle. Ping jumped off with a flutter of wings.

Dame Fuddle beamed. "My dear!" she said. "That was quite an entrance!"

"I do my best," Ping said.

The St Juniper fairies clapped enthusiastically. Nettle noticed that Brilliance was clapping more enthusiastically than anyone else.

"And what is your name, my dear?" Dame Fuddle asked.

"Pong," said Ping.

Nettle grinned. Then she remembered that she didn't like Ping, and stopped.

Dame Fuddle looked at the dragonfly. "And what is the name of your mount, Pong?"

"Ping," said Ping.

"Lovely!" Dame Fuddle said fondly.

The fairies clapped again.

A handsome elf stepped forward and made a flourishing bow. "My dear!" he said, smoothing back his long blond hair. "When I won the Midsummer Champion Butterfly Race, I was pitted against many talented riders. But none so talented as you!" He cleared his throat with a *hem-hem* noise. "Except for myself, of course."

"This is Lord Gallivant, *Ping*," said Dame Lacewing. "He is our butterfly riding teacher, and will take *Pong* to the stables."

"No thanks," said Ping. "I'm the only one who stables him. He bites everyone else."

Lord Gallivant stopped smiling.

"Did you say your name was Ping or Pong?" Dame Fuddle asked, looking confused.

"When's breakfast?" said Ping. "I'm starving."

"Of course!" said Dame Fuddle hurriedly. "Lord Gallivant will take you and your dragonfly to the stables straight away! Then we shall have a wonderful breakfast feast to welcome you to St Juniper's, Ping – Pong – my dear!"

2

Chinese Crackers

Nettle flew moodily down from the flowerpot tower. Everyone was queuing for breakfast outside the Dining Flowerpot. They were all talking about Ping's dramatic arrival.

"Did you see that amazing figure of eight over the Pond?" Tiptoe said.

"It looked more like a three to me," said Kelpie. Above her head, Flea was trying to fly backwards.

"Her dragonfly is amazing," Sesame said, looking dreamy. Sprout squeaked jealously.

"She is going to be my new best friend," Brilliance declared.

The others looked at each other and

rolled their eyes. They were used to
Brilliance.

Nettle scowled. "There was nothing
special about her."

"We're going to get on brilliantly,"
Brilliance said, ignoring Nettle. "I
can tell."

The Dining Flowerpot doors opened,
and the fairies streamed inside. A
special breakfast was laid out on the
food counters by the door: scrambled
ants' eggs, beech-nut sausages,
dandelion leaf salad, clover buns and
chicory coffee. Turnip the kitchen pixie
was standing behind the food counter
with his arms folded. "No pushing!" he
roared. "No shoving!"

"I love it when a new fairy comes to
St Juniper's," said Tiptoe happily, as
she piled her plate high with scrambled
ants' eggs.

"I wish Lord Gallivant would bring
Ping back from the stables," Brilliance

said. "I want her to sit with us."

"She'll have to sit with the teachers first," said Sesame.

The fairies looked at the long bark table at the far end of the Dining

Flowerpot, where the teachers of St Juniper's ate their meals.

Dame Fuddle was in the middle, with a mountain of beech-nut sausages on her plate. There was an empty chair next to her for Ping, decorated with a sprig of honeysuckle.

Dame Lacewing was sipping a cup of chicory coffee and looking thoughtful. Her pet beetle Pipsqueak sat at her feet.

Dame Honey, the Fairy English teacher, was making a tower of clover buns on her plate. She was giggling with Dame Taffeta, the Fairy Science teacher, every time the tower fell down.

Bindweed the garden pixie was quietly feeding dandelion leaves to his leaf-cutting ants under the table.

Legless the school earthworm was asleep under Lord Gallivant's empty chair.

"They're here!" Sesame squeaked with excitement.

Lord Gallivant and Ping were
standing in the Dining Flowerpot
doorway.

"We at St Juniper's welcome . . .
Pong!" Lord Gallivant said loudly.

Ping sniffed the air and looked puzzled. "I can't smell anything, Lord Gallivant," she said.

Dame Lacewing rapped her wand on the long bark table as the fairies giggled. "That's enough," she said sharply. "Lord Gallivant, bring our new pupil to the table."

Ping climbed the steps and sat down in the honeysuckle chair next to Dame Fuddle. She stared at her plate. "We don't eat ants' eggs in China," she told them. "We eat lotus leaves and cherry blossom pie."

Dame Fuddle looked anxious. "Do you mind eating ants' eggs, just this once?"

"I will eat them for *you*," Ping said graciously. She ate an ant's egg very daintily. Then she burped.

Dame Lacewing frowned.

Ping opened her eyes wide. "I'm sorry," she said. "I've never eaten an

ant's egg before. Perhaps it disagrees
with me."

"She did that on purpose," Nettle
hissed at Kelpie.

"Isn't she fantastic?" Brilliance breathed. "I'm going to ask Dame Fuddle if she can share our dormitory."

"Oooh, yes!" said Tiptoe.

"Can she sleep next to me?" said Sesame.

"I can teach her how to burp," said Kelpie.

"She can do that already," Nettle said sourly.

"That wasn't a burp," said Kelpie. "*This* is a burp."

Kelpie burped so loudly that she fell off her chair. Some fairies sitting nearby started clapping. Ping looked at the Naughty Fairies' table with interest.

Brillance put up her hand. "Dame Fuddle?" she said. "Can Ping come and sit with us? We'll look after her. I'm sure we can fit an extra bed into our dormitory."

"I don't think that's a good idea," Dame Lacewing began.

But Dame Fuddle beamed. "What a
kind thought, Brilliance," she said.
"Would you like that, Ping?"

"Sure," said Ping with a shrug.
Brilliance put down her hand.

"Brilliant," she said happily.

Nettle pushed away her dandelion leaf salad. She'd lost her appetite.

Ping sauntered down the Dining Flowerpot towards their table.

Brilliance gave Ping a brilliant smile. "Sit next to me, Ping," she said.

"I'll sit where I like," said Ping. She sat next to Brilliance.

"That was fantastic flying," said Sesame. "Did you get your Emperor dragonfly in China?"

"What do lotus leaves taste like?" Tiptoe asked.

"Don't know," said Ping. "I've never been to China."

"But you said . . ." Brilliance began.

Ping grinned. "I say a lot of things," she said. "Watch this."

She pulled a tiny black seed from her pocket and threw it casually across the room. It hit Dame Fuddle's plate of beech-nut sausages, which exploded in

a cloud of black smoke.

Dame Fuddle rose to her feet, her face black with soot, shouting, "Run for your lives! We're being attacked!"

All the fairies started yelling. Lord Gallivant fainted. Dame Taffeta screamed and jumped to her feet, knocking over Dame Honey's tower of clover buns. Pipsqueak sped out of the room on his short beetle legs. Even Legless moved, a bit.

"I believe Ping has another explanation, Dame Fuddle," said Dame Lacewing, her eyes boring into Ping.

The fairies quietened down as Ping stood up. "It's a traditional Chinese seed cracker," she said, sounding hurt. "Didn't you like it? We throw them to wish good luck."

Dame Fuddle wiped the soot from her nose and tried to smile. "That's . . . that's very nice, Pong," she said. "Traditional, is it? Lovely! But perhaps

. . . not indoors in future?"

The Naughty Fairies stared at the staff table, waiting for Dame Fuddle to give Ping a detention. But Dame Fuddle had sat down again, and was now eating the only unexploded beech-nut sausage left on her plate.

Dame Lacewing looked astonished.

"How did you do that?" Tiptoe asked in amazement.

"Traditions never get detentions," said Ping.

"That wasn't a tradition," Nettle said. "That was just a very loud bang."

Ping smirked.

"Totally brilliant," Brilliance said.

"Twinkle-tastic," Sesame sighed, and gave Sprout a dandelion leaf.

"Pretty good," said Kelpie.

Nettle stared. She'd hardly ever heard Kelpie say anything nice before.

What was wrong with her friends? They were all staring at Ping like she was an enormous sugared buttercup.

A hard lump formed in Nettle's heart.

   Ping wasn't a buttercup.

   She was a big, fat thorn.

3

Ping's Wand

The bluebells rang for the first lesson of the day. Nettle silently followed the others as they headed for Fairy English. The English Flowerpot overlooked the school Strawberry Patch at the back of St Juniper's.

"You'll like Dame Honey," Brilliance told Ping as they walked across the courtyard.

"I hate teachers," said Ping. "And teachers hate me."

"I hate Fairy English," said Sesame gloomily. Sprout squeaked in sympathy.

"That's because you're rubbish at it," said Kelpie. She threw a clover bun in the air for Flea, who was trying a figure of eight above the courtyard.

Dame Honey's flowerpot was bright
and colourful with enchanted petals,
which hovered in the air like birds.
Dame Honey was nearly as colourful as
the petals, with her ivy-leaf trousers
and pink cobweb top. She wore
pennyroyal slippers on her feet, and
starflowers in her hair. On Dame
Honey's desk there was a pile of dried
daisy petal paper and a grass cage full
of wriggling black dots.

"Help yourself to petal paper," Dame
Honey said as the fairies came into the
flowerpot. "Pollen ink in the cupboard.
I hope you're feeling energetic this
morning."

She pointed at a chalk sentence on
the rockboard behind her.

Imps said fairies are real stupid

"Where's the imp who said that?"

Kelpie bellowed, staring around the
classroom. "I'll show him who's stupid."

Dame Honey smiled. She opened the
grass cage and the squiggly black dots
flew into the air, forming a cloud.

All the fairies tried to jump up and

catch a black dot. But they were flying too fast.

"They're really sweet!" said Sesame, her eyes shining. "What are they, Dame Honey?"

"Commas," said Dame Honey. She waved her wand in a neat circle. "*Virgula!*"

A tiny black comma flew down and perched on the tip of Dame Honey's wand. Dame Honey put the comma carefully on the rockboard.

The sentence on the board now said:

Imps said fairies are real, stupid

"Course we're real," said Ping. "Everyone knows that."

The comma buzzed off the board and joined the rest of the commas near the flowerpot ceiling.

"Copy this sentence on to a piece of petal paper," said Dame Honey.

The fairies bent their heads over their bark desks and scribbled the sentence.

"Now," said Dame Honey. "Has everyone got their wands? I want you to catch more commas and change the sentence again. The magic word is *virgula*. Use your wands carefully, now. You only want one comma at a time."

Everyone pulled out their wands in excitement and started waving them at the commas. Tiptoe had a piece of honeycake stuck to her wand. Kelpie's was painted with yellow and black stripes. Sesame's had a baby earwig clinging to it, and Nettle's was covered with mud.

"*Verruca!*" Brilliance shouted, pointing at a comma. It whizzed past.

For the first time since she arrived at St Juniper's, Ping looked worried.

"What's the matter?" Brilliance asked.

"I can't find my wand!" said Ping.

Nettle suddenly remembered the flash of silver she'd seen falling into the

Pond. She opened her mouth. Then she closed it again.

Why should she tell Ping anything?

"You've lost your wand?" Dame

Honey asked, looking sympathetic. "Use this one for now." She handed Ping a school wand. It was a bit bent in the middle.

"Watch this," Ping whispered to the others.

From where Nettle was sitting, it looked like Ping was aiming her school wand out of the window at the Strawberry Patch.

A strawberry zoomed through the window. Several fairies ducked as the strawberry splattered against the flowerpot wall.

Ping opened her eyes wide. "Whoops," she said.

"Never mind," said Dame Honey cheerfully. "School wands sometimes need tuning. Try aiming to the left of the commas, instead of straight at them."

"You did that on purpose," Nettle accused her.

"So?" Ping challenged.

The tension was broken by Tiptoe. "Look!" she squeaked. "I made another sentence!"

"Brilliant," said Brilliance. But she wasn't looking at Tiptoe's sentence. She was looking at Ping with stars in her eyes.

Nettle muttered *"Virgula!"* and pointed her wand at the commas so hard that the whole cloud zoomed down and knocked her over.

After Fairy English, they had Butterfly Riding with Lord Gallivant.

"This is my favourite lesson," said Brilliance happily, walking with her arm linked through Ping's. "I'm brilliant at flying."

"I bet you're not as brilliant as me," said Ping.

Sprout suddenly gave a shrill squeak.

"Watch where you're going, Nettle!" Sesame said. "You stepped on Sprout's tail!"

It had started to rain. Lord Gallivant
was waiting for them at the Butterfly
Stables on the back of his Red Admiral
butterfly, Plankton. The school Cabbage
White butterflies were waiting patiently
in their butterfly stalls.

"Greetings, young fairies!" he said, smoothing his hair. "A good morning to test your rain-flying skills. This, of course, is nothing. When I won the Midsummer Champion Butterfly Race, we had a typhoon."

The wind was blowing at the fairies and fluttering their wings. It was hard to stand upright.

"First, we shall race to the Hedge," said Lord Gallivant, as the fairies pulled the school butterflies out of their stalls.

Ping remained where she was. "I want to ride Pong," she said.

Lord Gallivant wagged a finger at her. "This is butterfly riding," he said. "No dragonflies today."

Ping opened her eyes wide. "I bet you're really good at flying, Lord Gallivant," she said. "I'd love to race you. You'd probably beat me, even though I'm on a dragonfly."

Lord Gallivant looked delighted. "I'm

never one to boast," he said, crinkling his eyes at Ping, "but that would be an interesting race. Very well. You may ride your dragonfly today."

As the other fairies mounted their butterflies, Ping swooped out of the stables on Pong. Pong's blue scales looked almost black in the rain.

"Ping's amazing at getting what she wants," said Tiptoe wistfully. She was sitting on the back of Snowball, the biggest and most ragged school butterfly in the stables. Snowball's wings were see-through in the rain.

Sesame stroked Ice, her school butterfly, and rose off the ground. "Do you think Ping might let me ride Pong one day?" she asked. On the stable floor below, Sprout squeaked mournfully.

Brilliance clicked her tongue at her butterfly, Ivory. "I bet Ping beats Lord Gallivant," she said. "Come on. I want to get a good view of the race."

"How come she gets to ride Pong
when I can't ride Flea?" Kelpie
demanded, looking sulky on the back of
a school butterfly called Chalky.

"Because she's totally brilliant," said
Nettle bitterly.

"Ping's OK, you know," Kelpie said.

"You should give her a chance."

"Huh!" Nettle said. "That stupid stuff with the school wand in Dame Honey's class. She's such a show-off."

"She's going to be in trouble if she doesn't find her own wand soon," said Kelpie, rising unsteadily on Chalky's back. "We've got Fairy Maths this afternoon. Dame Lacewing is very strict about looking after your wand."

"Huh," said Nettle again. She kicked her butterfly, Salt, and rose high up into the wet air.

4

Fairy Maths

Lunch was Nettle's favourite: rose-hip pie and strawberry juice. The Naughty Fairies sat together at their usual bark table. Nettle sat as far away from Ping and Brilliance as she could.

"Lord Gallivant didn't say much after the race, did he?" Brilliance said happily, slurping her strawberry juice.

"He's just a bad loser," said Ping with a shrug. She had made it back to the butterfly stables before Lord Gallivant had even reached the Hedge. The butterfly riding instructor had been in a mood for the rest of the lesson.

"Pong's five times bigger than Plankton," Nettle muttered.

"It was brilliant flying," said Brilliance warmly.

"Thanks," said Ping. She finished her rose-hip pie in one bite. "Anyone want some more?"

Nettle's mouth watered. But she kept her lips tightly shut.

Ping looked at Nettle and smiled. Then she stood up and walked over to the food counter.

There was a bang, and a shout. The fairies turned round to see Turnip the kitchen pixie staring at his kitchen spoon. For some reason, it had turned into a tiny, bad-tempered dragon.

Ping sauntered back to the Naughty Fairies' table with a second helping of rose-hip pie.

"Was that you?" Tiptoe gasped.

"Maybe," said Ping.

Turnip let out a roar of anger as the tiny dragon clamped its teeth on the end of his nose.

"How did you do it?" Kelpie asked curiously.

"Who says I did it?" said Ping.

"It looks like Turnip suspects you," said Nettle. "He hates practical jokes."

The kitchen pixie was staring ferociously in Ping's direction. He was holding the tiny dragon by its tail. The dragon swung from side to side trying to bite him.

"He can't prove I did it," said Ping after a pause. But she sounded uncomfortable.

The dragon turned back into a spoon. Without taking his eyes off Ping, Turnip put the spoon in his pocket.

"You'd better not get a detention any time soon, Ping," Brilliance said. "Turnip takes them, and he has a long memory."

"I never get detentions," said Ping. She pushed away the remains of her rose-hip pie.

Nettle thought of Ping's missing wand and Fairy Maths with Dame Lacewing that afternoon, and smiled. "Can I have the rest of your pie, Ping?" she asked sweetly. "Seems a shame to waste it."

After lunch, Sesame turned hopefully to Ping.

"Could I – would you let me ride Pong, Ping?" she asked. "We can ride butterflies at lunchtime before lessons, and I was just wondering . . ."

Ping frowned. "No one rides Pong except for me," she said.

"Oh," said Sesame, looking crestfallen.

"You can help me feed him, if you like," Ping offered. "We can go to the stables now."

Sesame beamed. Sprout squeaked grumpily.

"Shouldn't you look for your wand,

Ping?" asked Tiptoe. "It's Fairy Maths this afternoon."

"Boring," Brilliance yawned.

"You might get a detention if you don't find it," Nettle said casually.

"Pong's more important," said Ping. "Anyone else coming?"

Brilliance, Tiptoe and Sesame walked with Ping across the courtyard, towards the Butterfly Stables.

"Are you coming, Nettle?" Kelpie asked.

"No," said Nettle.

Kelpie shrugged. "Suit yourself."

Flea swooped over Nettle's head and followed Kelpie. Nettle stared after her friends. A little voice started up in her head.

Tell Ping that her wand's in the Pond.

"No," said Nettle loudly. "I won't." And she marched off to the Sports Field to bounce on the cobweb trampoline and pretend that she was bouncing on

Ping's head. Or maybe Brilliance's head. Or maybe both.

"Take your seats," said Dame Lacewing. "We have a lot to do today."

The Maths Flowerpot was tall and dark, and stood next to the staffroom at the back of the school. There were complicated number charts on the walls. A large abacus made of dried

seeds stood by the door. COME-TO-ME
CHARMS was written in big chalk
letters on the rockboard. Pipsqueak,
Dame Lacewing's beetle, stood
importantly by the door as the fairies
came into the flowerpot.

Dame Lacewing looked at Nettle and
the others. They were walking with
Ping to their usual places at the back.

"You six will sit at the front today,
please," she said.

"But Dame Lacewing," said Ping. "I
have to sit at the back."

"Do you," said Dame Lacewing.

"Oh yes," said Ping. "It's my seeing
problem, you see. I can only see things
from far away."

Dame Lacewing smiled like a wasp
looking at a juicy raspberry. She waved
her wand. There was a pop, and a large
and unflattering pair of spectacles
appeared on Ping's nose. Ping tried to
take the spectacles off, but they were

firmly fixed in place.

"Better?" Dame Lacewing asked.

Ping glared at her.

"Good," said Dame Lacewing. "At the front, please."

The Naughty Fairies sat in the front row. The spectacles vanished from Ping's nose with a backwards-sounding pop.

"Come-to-me charms," said Dame Lacewing, "need concentration and accurate measurements."

Brilliance put up her hand. "Dame Lacewing? Dame Honey taught us a come-to-me charm this morning. Can't we just use that?"

"Dame Honey's charm may bring you commas," Dame Lacewing said, tapping her wand on her hand, "but you need a stronger charm for anything bigger. First, you must measure your object." She picked up Pipsqueak and set him on the desk. She flicked her wand around him twice, and then put him down again. "Back of the flowerpot, Pipsqueak," she said.

Pipsqueak trotted obediently to the back of the flowerpot.

"Pipsqueak is five millisquirts wide, and seven millisquirts long," said Dame Lacewing. She wrote "5" and "7" on the blackboard. "Can anyone tell me what we do next?"

"Die of boredom?" Ping whispered to Nettle.

"I can hear most whispers, Ping," said Dame Lacewing. "I only give one warning and then I give you a detention. This is your warning."

"Fine!" said Ping crossly. She folded her arms.

"Tiptoe," said Dame Lacewing. "Spit out that dew chew and come up here."

Tiptoe went up to Dame Lacewing's desk.

"Multiply five and seven," said Dame Lacewing. "You may use the abacus."

Tiptoe moved five dried seeds across the abacus. Then she moved seven more. "Ten," she said after a minute.

"If you summoned Pipsqueak on that basis, " said Dame Lacewing, "you'd get his legs, but not much else."

Pipsqueak honked nervously.

"The answer is thirty-five," said Dame Lacewing. She traced a sparkling number 35 in the air with her wand.

"*Andeca!*" she commanded, as the
sparkling numbers faded away.

Pipsqueak floated up the classroom
and landed lightly on Dame Lacewing's
desk. The fairies started chattering with
interest. Dame Lacewing put Pipsqueak
on the floor and placed a bowl of ants'
eggs on her desk.

"These ants' eggs are two millisquirts long, and one millisquirt wide," she said. "That makes . . . ?"

"A very small omelette," Kelpie suggested.

The fairies giggled. Dame Lacewing sighed. "Two," she said. "I want you to trace the number two in the air with your wand. Say the magic word *andeca*, and think very hard about the eggs. You must summon just one, and you must not break it. We shall do this a row at a time. Front row, please."

Brilliance summoned her egg and caught it neatly in mid-air. Nettle's egg flew over her head and landed on the floor. Kelpie managed to summon three at once, while Sesame couldn't move the eggs at all. Tiptoe added an extra wiggle to her number two by mistake, and covered herself with yolk.

Ping raised her school wand and swirled a lazy number two. *"Andela!"*

Nettle saw Ping twitch her wrist. The egg rose into the air, swerved and smacked straight into Dame Lacewing.

"Whoops," said Ping, opening her eyes wide. "Sorry, Dame Lacewing. This school wand is a bit bent."

Nettle couldn't help laughing. Ping winked at her. Nettle looked away quickly.

Dame Lacewing wiped the egg yolk off her forehead. "Where is your own wand, Ping?" she said in a dangerous-sounding voice.

"I don't know, Dame Lacewing," said Ping.

"Detention with Turnip in the kitchen tonight," said Dame Lacewing sharply. "And if you have not found your wand by tomorrow lunchtime, Turnip will expect you in the kitchens every evening for the rest of the week!"

5

Out of Bounds

There was an extra bed in the Naughty Fairies' dormitory that evening.

"Sleep next to me, Ping!" said Brilliance.

"Me!" Tiptoe squeaked.

"Me and Sprout!" said Sesame, cuddling Sprout.

"You'd better not snore," Kelpie said. "You'll wake up Flea." She stroked Flea, who was curled up on the dormitory window sill.

Nettle flopped down on her foxglove sleeping bag and buried her face in her wool pillow. *I don't care where Ping sleeps*, she told herself.

"I'll sleep where I like," said Ping.

She sat down on the bed next to Nettle.
"But I'm not going to sleep tonight."

"Why not?" asked Sesame in surprise.

"Because I have to find my wand!"
Ping said. "Turnip made me feed the
school maggots tonight."

"Yuk!"

The St Juniper's maggots ate the school waste and kept the kitchen bins clean. Turnip said they were very friendly, but their shiny white bodies and blind faces always made the fairies shudder.

"There's no way I'm doing detention with him all week," said Ping.

"Where did you last see your wand?" Brilliance asked.

"I think I had it when I arrived this morning," said Ping, "but I'm not sure."

"We need a plan," Brilliance announced.

"How about Dame Lacewing's come-to-me charm?" Tiptoe suggested.

Ping pulled out her school wand. Sesame ducked. "Don't worry, Sesame," said Ping. "It works perfectly fine. Now, my wand's about three millisquirts long, and a quarter of a millisquirt wide. How much is that?"

The fairies were silent.

"Three-quarters," said Nettle, looking up from her pillow.

"Thanks," said Ping. She closed her eyes and traced ¾ in the air with the wand. "*Andeca!*"

"Ow," said Tiptoe.

Nettle's wand had jumped up and hit Tiptoe on the head.

"We have to be closer to it to summon it," Brilliance guessed.

Tiptoe rubbed her head. "But we don't know where it is," she said.

Brilliance waved her hand impatiently. "Details," she said.

Ping put down her school wand. "That's it," she said in a doomed voice. "My life is over."

"It's only a couple of detentions," said Kelpie scornfully.

"It's a couple of detentions with Turnip and those maggots," said Ping. "He hates me! Listen," she said after a

moment. "Whoever finds my wand can
have a ride on Pong."

"Really?" Sesame gasped.

"Wow," said Tiptoe.

"I'll find it," said Brilliance
confidently.

"I don't like dragonflies," said Kelpie.

"Nettle?" said Ping.

"What?" said Nettle, putting her ear spiders on her bedside table.

"Will you help?" Ping asked. "Please?"

Nettle thought of the wand in the Pond. "Why should I?" she said.

"Because maybe you like me, just a bit?" Ping suggested hopefully.

"Who says I like you?" said Nettle, and turned to face the wall. She was going to find Ping's wand all right. But she was going to do it alone.

Nettle woke up suddenly. One of her ear spiders was gently tickling her neck. She sat up in bed and rubbed her eyes and yawned.

Dawn was beginning to creep into the sky. The other fairies were still asleep. Nettle got out of bed as quietly as she could. Flea gave a sleepy buzz from the window sill as she crept over him and

launched herself into the air.

Nettle loved flying. She twirled in the brightening sky, feeling the dew on her cheeks and the wind in her hair. Then she swooped towards the blackberry bushes between St Juniper's and the Pond. She landed lightly on a leaf next to a large blackberry.

"Breakfast first, wand second," Nettle said to herself. She took a bite of the blackberry. Then she stared at the Pond ahead. It was much bigger than Nettle remembered. She felt her stomach sink. This wasn't going to be easy.

She thought of Pong's gleaming blue scales and his whirring wings. She really wanted to ride him. She especially wanted to ride him before Brilliance did.

Nettle finished the blackberry. She washed her sticky face and hands in a dewdrop that was shimmering on the leaf beside her. Then at last she flew down to the water's edge.

Rocks and reeds stood high above her. Pond water sloshed at her toes. Nettle pulled out her wand and drew a ¾ in

the air. *"Andeca?"* she said hopefully.

A twig twitched at her feet. Nettle stepped on it quickly, to stop it from jumping up and hitting her on the head. She wasn't close enough to the wand. Nettle stared at the wide Pond and wondered if she should try and swim across it. She'd never swum before.

The water blopped and shivered, and an enormous shiny green head popped up. Terrified, Nettle stared into two bright yellow eyes.

The frog croaked at her.

"Um," said Nettle, trying not to shake. "Hello. I'm not a fly, by the way. In case you were wondering."

The frog croaked again. Nettle suddenly had an idea. "Please," she said. It came out as a whisper, and she cleared her throat. "Please," she said again, "I need a lift out into the middle of the Pond, and . . . um . . ."

The frog blinked. Then it crawled out
of the water and sat quietly on a nearby
rock. Nettle flew up and settled on the
frog's back. It was cold and wet and
slippery, and almost impossible to hold
on to. Nettle clamped her legs around

the frog as hard as she could, and
closed her eyes.

There was a splosh and a rocking-
rolling sensation. Nettle opened her

eyes. The frog was swimming with its head above water, kicking with its strong back legs. It was heading for a large lilypad in the middle of the Pond.

As the frog swam along, Nettle peered down into the green water, looking for Ping's wand. Pondweed waved underneath the surface. There was a gleam of curly water snails and enormous golden fish far below. Nettle wanted to reach for her wand and sketch a ¾ in the air again, but she didn't dare to let go of the frog's back.

"I'll wait until we reach the lilypad," Nettle decided.

As the frog neared the lilypad, a shadow fell across the water and blotted out the sun. Nettle looked up – up and up and up – until she could see, far above the water, the enormous, spearlike head of a heron.

The heron darted. Nettle flung her arms around the frog and screamed.

And the frog gave an almighty kick and sank far below the surface, pulling Nettle down with him.

She felt the frog slipping away – she couldn't hold on any longer.

6

Water Wings

The heron speared the water, and the frog twisted away just in time. Nettle sank out of the heron's reach.

Nettle stared around in terror, in the pale green light under the water. Everything was still and quiet and cold. Nettle sank down and down – right to the bottom of the Pond. This wasn't right! This was all completely wrong! She had to go up, she had to breathe, she had to fly away from here, forget Ping's wand, forget . . .

A slim silver wand lay gleaming on the muddy Pond floor. Nettle wanted to cry with relief. She waved her wand clumsily in the water.

"*An*-blop-*de*-blup-*ca!*"

Very slowly, the silver wand lifted from the mud and floated through the water towards Nettle. As Nettle reached for it, the frog swam past her and disappeared.

Holding tightly to both wands, Nettle kicked her legs like the frog had done. She started rising in the water. This was like flying! She tried to flap her wings, but they wouldn't move. Nettle concentrated on kicking – through the weed, past the water snails, up to where the light changed from pale green to white. With a *plop*, she pushed her face out of the water. Air had never tasted so delicious.

Swimming up had been easy. Staying up was different. Nettle kicked, splashed and flapped her wet wings, but she couldn't lift herself from the Pond.

With relief, Nettle suddenly spotted a fat green lilypad. She grabbed it and

pulled herself out of the water. Nettle
held on to the lilypad and waited for
her heart to stop pounding.

I'm safe, she thought. *And I've got*

Ping's wand! She could feel Pong's smooth blue sides against her knees already. Brilliance would be friends with her again. Maybe Ping would be friends with her too.

Nettle put her wet and shivering ear spiders on the lilypad to dry. Then she tested her wings.

Her wings stayed stuck to her back.

She tested them again. But they wouldn't move.

Nettle reached around and felt her wings anxiously. They were soaking wet.

She stared across the Pond to the distant shore. She couldn't fly. She could swim a bit, but not that far. There was no sign of the frog.

How was she going to get back to the shore?

Think, Nettle told herself. *You're good at ideas, whatever Brilliance says.*

A group of pond skaters zigzagged merrily past the lilypad. "Wait!" Nettle called. "Please!"

The pond skaters stopped. They waved their antenna cheerfully at Nettle. And Nettle had a fantastic idea,

followed by an even more fantastic
plan.

"I need some silk," she told her
ear spiders.

The spiders obediently spun two long
pieces of silk as Nettle climbed on to
the lilypad. She twisted the silk
together to make a rope and holding
the ends, she looped it underneath the
lilypad. She tugged until she felt the
rope touch the lilypad stem. Then she
started sawing.

Back and forth, back and forth. Nettle
sawed steadily, pulling one end of the

silk rope and then the other. The pond skaters watched with interest. Nettle's arms started to ache, but she kept sawing until . . .

The stem of the lilypad snapped. After tucking both wands into her belt, Nettle pulled the silk rope out of the water. She looped the middle section of rope around four of the pond skaters. Then she took the ends and shook them like a pair of reins.

The pond skaters began to move,

pulling Nettle and the lilypad behind them. Nettle gave a yell of triumph. She planted her feet firmly on the lilypad and steered the pond skaters towards the shore.

The long black shadow of a hungry fish glided far below. It stared up at the moving lilypad with flat fishy eyes.

Back at St Juniper's, the other fairies were waking up.

"Sit next to me at breakfast," Brilliance said, plonking herself down on Ping's bed.

"I'll sit where I like," said Ping, rubbing her eyes and yawning. "Where's Nettle?"

The fairies all stared at Nettle's empty bed.

"That's odd," said Sesame, washing Sprout's face in the walnut shell by the door. Sprout squeaked miserably.

"Do you think she's OK?" Tiptoe

asked. "She was behaving strangely yesterday."

"Nettle, Nettle, Nettle," said Brilliance crossly. "Why do we always talk about Nettle?"

"We didn't talk about her yesterday at all," said Kelpie, brushing Flea's fur with her hair thistle. "You didn't even talk *to* her, Brilliance."

"Did you have an argument with Nettle yesterday, Brilliance?" Ping asked. "What happened?"

"Let's go to breakfast," said Brilliance loudly. She jumped off the bed and marched to the dormitory door. "Anyone coming?"

Kelpie put down her hair thistle. Flea buzzed grumpily at her. "Tell Ping what happened on the highest flowerpot tower yesterday, Brilliance," she said.

Brilliance rolled her eyes. "Nettle freaked at me when I had this totally brilliant idea," she began.

"Nettle had the idea," said Tiptoe.

"Idea, plan – what's the difference?" said Brilliance.

"What was the idea?" Ping asked.

"Raindrop bombs," said Brilliance. "Anyone could have thought of them."

"*Anyone* didn't," said Kelpie. "Nettle did."

Brilliance fell silent.

"Nettle was alone on the flowerpot tower when I arrived," said Ping. "She looked pretty cross about something. So I did my backwards figure of eight over the Pond to cheer her up and— *Oh!*"

"What?" said Brilliance grumpily.

The other fairies stared at Ping, who had suddenly jumped out of her foxglove sleeping bag.

"I just remembered!" Ping gasped. "I felt something fall when I was doing the figure of eight – Nettle must have seen me drop it – my wand's in the Pond and Nettle's gone to find it!"

"Why would she do that?" Kelpie asked. "She doesn't like you."

"Yes she does," Ping said stubbornly. "She helped work out my wand's millisquirt measurement, didn't she?"

This was true.

"Has Nettle really gone to the Pond on her own?" Sesame was scared. "It's so big and wet and . . . there are things there that eat fairies. I'm sure of it."

"Nettle's a daredevil," said Tiptoe. "She's never scared of anything."

"Cover for me at breakfast," Ping announced. "I'm going to the Pond to find my wand. And maybe I'll find Nettle as well."

"You're not," said Brilliance, after a moment. "We have this rule. Naughty Fairies always do stuff together."

"After NFing," Kelpie added.

Ping looked confused.

"We all say something beginning with NF, like Naughty Fairies," Tiptoe explained.

"I'm not very good at it," Sesame said sheepishly.

"It's our code," said Brilliance. "So – Naughty Fairies!" She put out her fist.

"Nippy flotsam," said Kelpie. She put

her fist on top of Brilliance's.

"Nutlet fountain!" Tiptoe said.

"Numbskull phantom?" Sesame
offered.

"Phantom's spelt with a 'ph'," Ping
said.

"Told you I wasn't very good," said
Sesame gloomily.

"Numbered fangs," Ping said. "How's
that?"

"Not bad," Brilliance said. "Look, I
know I've been a bit funny with Nettle
since that raindrop bomb thing—"

"A bit?" Kelpie said.

Brilliance had the grace to blush.
"OK, more than a bit. But she's my
friend and I'd never leave her all on
her own somewhere like the Pond. So –
fly, fly . . ."

"To the SKY!" the other fairies
chanted, and lifted their piled fists into
the air.

"We can all ride over there on Pong,"

Sesame added, with a hopeful glance at Ping.

"That might not be much fun," said Ping after a moment.

"Who says?" Kelpie demanded.

Ping grinned wickedly. "Pong bites."

7

Fish Breath

Nettle started whistling as she pulled the reins to the left. She'd never whistled before, but it felt like a good time to start.

The shore was getting nearer. Nettle thought happily about riding Pong. There was a dragonfly zooming across the Pond towards her. Was Pong as big as that? She couldn't remember.

The dragonfly stopped and hovered above Nettle and the lilypad.

"Hey!" Ping shouted down at Nettle. "Did you find my wand?"

Nettle almost dropped the reins. Ping and her four friends were staring down at her from Pong's back. Sesame and

Tiptoe were stroking Pong's blue scales. Sprout's head peeped mournfully out of the neck of Sesame's dress. Kelpie was lying full stretch down Pong's long back, with her hands behind her head. Brilliance was staring at the sky, looking a bit embarrassed.

"What are you doing here?" Nettle demanded.

"We've come to see if you're OK," Tiptoe shouted.

Nettle thought about the frog, and the heron, and the deep cold water, and her wet wings. "Why wouldn't I be OK?" she said.

"Did you find my wand?" Ping asked again.

"Yes." Nettle clicked her tongue at the pond skaters, who speeded up. Ping dug her knees into Pong's sides, and the dragonfly speeded up as well.

"Why are you running away?" Ping asked her.

"I'm not running," said Nettle. "I'm waterskiing."

Kelpie propped herself up on one elbow. "Why aren't you flying?" she asked.

"My wings got wet," said Nettle.

"How did you make the lilypad sail along like that?" Tiptoe asked admiringly.

Nettle glared up at Brilliance. "I had an idea," she said. "And then I had a plan. I'm funny that way."

The fairies all looked at Brilliance.

"Sorry for taking your idea about the raindrop bombs, Nettle," said Brilliance. "It's just – my plan was kind of brilliant."

"So was my idea," Nettle shot back.

"I know," said Brilliance. "I only make plans for brilliant ideas. That's why we make a brilliant team."

"Friends again?" asked Ping.

"All right," said Nettle. Brilliance

beamed down at her.

"What's that shadow underneath your lilypad, Nettle?" Sesame asked.

Everything happened at once. The fish jumped out of the water with its

mouth open – Ping pulled Nettle on to Pong's back – Sesame screamed – Pong rocketed up to the sky – and the fish crashed back into the pond with a mighty splash.

"Is everyone OK?" Nettle gasped, as Pong pelted away from the pond in terror.

Sprout gave a muffled squeak from inside Sesame's dress.

"Fine," panted Sesame and Tiptoe.

"Brilliant," panted Brilliance.

"Wet," said Kelpie in disgust.

Nettle stared around in panic. Ping wasn't sitting on Pong's back.

"Ping?" she called. "Where are you?"

Why had she been so horrible to Ping? Ping was cool, and funny, and naughty. Nettle wanted to be her friend more than anything. But maybe it was too late! Maybe . . .

"Ping!" she yelled despairingly.

"Poo," said Ping, plopping down on

Pong's back with a whirr of lilac wings. "That fish had the worst breath."

"You're OK?" Nettle stuttered. "You're OK! Oh Ping, I'm so glad you're OK!"

"Did you go right inside the fish?" Sesame gasped.

"Yuk!" Tiptoe gave a shudder.

"Totally gross," Kelpie said with a grin.

"Just brilliant," Brilliance sighed.

"That was nothing," Ping said modestly. "Watch this . . ."

And she shot up into the sky and did four somersaults in a row.

"Good one, Ping!" Nettle shouted. "You'll have to teach me that!"

"Any time, Nettle!" Ping shouted back. "Any time!"

Imps are Wimps

Fairy Science is just NOT cool.

So when the Naughty Fairies face a science test they need some magic help.

But what do imps and creepy crawlies have to do with it?

It's all part of Brilliance's brilliant plan . . .

Caterpillar Thriller

The Naughty Fairies have great plans to turn Dame Taffeta into a human catapult, and to beat Ambrosia Academy in the Butterfly Cup.

But nothing goes quite right.

They'll have to break every rule to win the fabulous Cup prize!

Sweet Cheat

The May Day Feast is coming . . .
   And that means Turnip the kitchen
pixie's TOFFEE!
   But what's his special ingredient?
   When greedy Tiptoe eats all his
toffee, she needs to find out – fast!